ENCYCLOPEDIA BROWN

THE CASE OF THE EXPLODING PLUMBING

and Other Mysteries

(hardcover title: *Encyclopedia Brown Lends a Hand*)

Also by Donald J. Sobol:

Encyclopedia Brown and The Case of the Dead Eagles

Encyclopedia Brown Carries On

Encyclopedia Brown Solves Them All

Angie's First Case

Other APPLE® PAPERBACKS you will want to read:

Casey and The Great Idea
by Joan Lowery Nixon

The Chicken Bone Wish
(hardcover title: *Joshua, the Czar, and the Chicken Bone Wish*)
by Barbara Girion

I Want to Go Home!
by Gordon Korman

The Magic Moscow
by Daniel Pinkwater

The Revenge of the Incredible Dr. Rancid and His Youthful Assistant, Jeffrey
by Ellen Conford

Wally
by Judie Wolkoff

ENCYCLOPEDIA BROWN

THE CASE OF THE EXPLODING PLUMBING and Other Mysteries

(hardcover title: *Encyclopedia Brown Lends a Hand*)

by

Donald J. Sobol

Illustrated by

Leonard Shortall

SCHOLASTIC INC.
New York Toronto London Auckland Sydney

For Cecy and Dick Rowen

ISBN 0-590-44093-4

 This edition published by Scholastic Inc., 730 Broadway, New York, NY 10003, by arrangement with Lodestar Books, a division of E.P. Dutton

12 11 10 9 8 7 6 5 2 3 4 5/9

Printed in the U.S.A. 40

Contents

The Case of the Runaway Elephant

ACROSS THE LENGTH and breadth of America people were wondering:

"What is Idaville's secret?"

For more than a year now, no one had gotten away with a crime in Idaville.

Aside from being a model of law and order, Idaville was a lovely seaside town. It had clean beaches and three movie theaters. It had churches, a synagogue, four banks, and two delicatessens.

The chief of police was Mr. Brown. He knew that nearly every American thought he was the best peace officer in the nation. He also knew the truth about Idaville.

The real brains behind Idaville's war on

crime was his only child, ten-year-old Encyclopedia.

Whenever Chief Brown had a mystery he could not solve, he put his emergency plan into action. He went home to dinner. At the table he told Encyclopedia the facts.

The boy detective solved the case before dessert. Once in a while, however, he had to ask for second helpings to gain more time.

Chief Brown hated keeping his son's ability a secret. He felt Congress should award Encyclopedia a vote of thanks. But how could he suggest it?

Who would believe that the guiding hand behind Idaville's police record could make a yo-yo loop-the-loop off a man-on-the-flying trapeze?

No one.

So Chief Brown said nothing.

Encyclopedia never let slip a word about the help he gave his father. He did not want to seem different from other fifth-graders.

But he was stuck with his nickname.

Only his parents and teachers called him by his right name, Leroy. Everyone else in Idaville called him Encyclopedia.

An encyclopedia is a book or set of books filled with facts from A to Z. Encyclopedia had read so many books he was really more like a library. You might say he was the only library in which the information desk was on the top floor.

One evening Chief Brown looked up from his soup. "Friday the thirteenth," he muttered.

"You're mistaken, dear," said Mrs. Brown. "Today is Friday the twelfth."

"I'm talking about seventeen years ago," said Chief Brown.

"Does the date have something to do with a case?" asked Encyclopedia.

"Yes, with Mr. Hunt's elephant, Jimbo," answered Chief Brown. "The animal is causing a problem."

Encyclopedia refused to believe his ears. Jimbo was the only pet elephant in Idaville. He never caused anyone a problem. Mr. Hunt kept him in the backyard.

"If Jimbo is in the middle of a mystery, tell Leroy," urged Mrs. Brown. "It could be his biggest case."

Chief Brown nodded. "It turns out that Jimbo may not belong to Mr. Hunt after all," he began. "Mr. Hunt found him outside his bedroom window on April Fools' Day seventeen years ago."

"What a shock for him!" exclaimed Mrs. Brown.

"I imagine so," replied Chief Brown. "Mr.

Hunt opened his eyes, and there was Jimbo peeping through the window. He woke up Mrs. Hunt to make sure he wasn't dreaming."

"What did she say?" asked Encyclopedia.

"'I hope he's on a leash,'" replied Chief Brown, "according to Mr. Hunt."

"Mr. Hunt has a great memory," marveled Encyclopedia.

"So does Mr. Xippas," said Chief Brown. "He came to my office today. He says he owns the elephant and wants him back. He claims Mr. Hunt never paid for Jimbo."

"What does Mr. Hunt say?" inquired Mrs. Brown.

"Mr. Hunt insists that he mailed the money to Mr. Xippas," said Chief Brown.

He waited while Mrs. Brown cleared the soup bowls. When she had served the ham loaf, he took his notebook from his breast pocket.

"I spoke with both Mr. Xippas and Mr. Hunt today," he said. "I'll give you Mr. Hunt's side first."

Encyclopedia and his mother listened as Chief Brown read from his notes.

"Mr. Hunt says that he thought the elephant in his backyard was a prank, since it was April Fools' Day. He immediately called the police. It turned out that the elephant had run away from a little circus which had just arrived in town.

"An hour later Mr. Xippas came to Mr. Hunt's house. Mr. Xippas owned and trained Jimbo. By then the Hunts had taken a liking to the animal. They asked Mr. Xippas if he would sell him.

"Mr. Xippas agreed. He also agreed to stay at the Hunts' house a week or two. The couple wanted to learn how to care for Jimbo. Mr. Xippas, however, asked to see their money first. So that afternoon Mr. Hunt drew the cash from the Oceanside Bank and showed it to the animal trainer.

"After nearly two weeks, the Hunts felt they could handle the friendly Jimbo. Mr. Hunt offered Mr. Xippas the money. Mr. Xippas wouldn't take it because it was Friday the thirteenth, which he said was bad luck for him.

"The same night Mr. Xippas left Idaville. He left a forwarding address, and Mr. Hunt mailed him the money."

Chief Brown looked up from his notebook.

"That's Mr. Hunt's story," he said. "Mr. Xippas insists he never got the money. The address was his sister's house in New Jersey. He says she was sick and had telephoned him to come and be with her."

"Why did Mr. Xippas wait seventeen years

before coming back to Idaville to claim Jimbo?" asked Encyclopedia. "It doesn't sound right."

"He says his sister died shortly after he reached her bedside," replied Chief Brown. "A day after her death, he got an offer of a job in India. He's been overseas all this time. He only returned to the United States five days ago."

"I wonder about him," said Mrs. Brown. "Why did he ask to see Mr. Hunt's money that very first day? I don't think that was nice. He should have trusted Mr. Hunt."

"Mr. Xippas says he didn't ask to see the money," answered Chief Brown. "He says Mr. Hunt never went to the bank. Furthermore, the only reason he stayed so long with the Hunts was that every day Mr. Hunt promised to pay him the following day."

Chief Brown closed his notebook.

"I should add," he said, "that Mr. Xippas denies that he refused the money on Friday the thirteenth because it was bad luck. He says the only thing Mr. Hunt gave him were promises to pay."

"What about the bank?" said Mrs. Brown. "Don't banks keep records?"

"A hurricane struck later that year," said Chief Brown. "It flooded the Oceanside Bank,

Mr. Hunt's home, and most of the buildings in Idaville. All the records were destroyed."

"I still don't understand something," said Mrs. Brown. "Mr. Xippas worked in the circus. How could he take nearly two weeks off to stay with the Hunts?"

"Mr. Xippas told me that he had become tired of circus life," said Chief Brown. "By selling Jimbo, he could quit and open his own business."

"Whom to believe?" sighed Mrs. Brown.

She had risen to clear the dishes and bring in the dessert. She glanced at Encyclopedia with concern. He always solved a case before dessert. Was this case too hard?

The boy detective closed his eyes. He always closed his eyes when he did his deepest thinking.

Suddenly his eyes opened. "Dad," he said. "Both men have memories like an elephant. But the one who is lying is Mr. ——"

WHO?

(Turn to page 64 for the solution to The Case of the Runaway Elephant.)

The Case of the Worn-Out Sayings

DURING THE SUMMER, Encyclopedia ran a detective agency in his garage. He wanted to help the children of the neighborhood.

Every morning he hung out his sign.

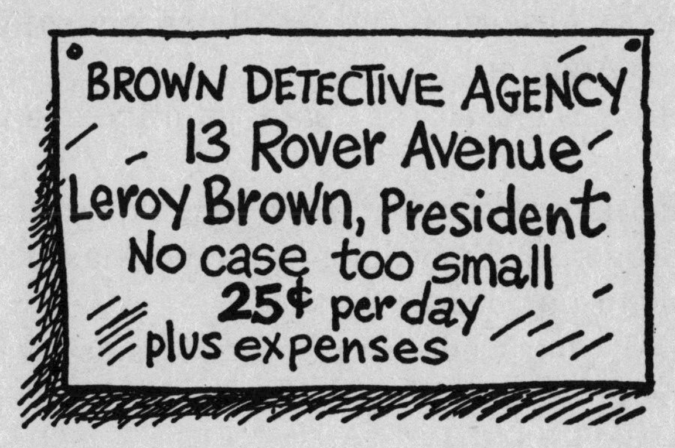

Thursday morning he received a telephone

call from Max Corrigan. Max was ten and needed help.

Encyclopedia biked to the corner of Maple and Main streets, where Max sat glumly behind a tableful of books. Above him was a beach umbrella on which was written: "All Kinds of Information — 5¢ to 15¢."

"I'm quitting this corner," announced Max. "It's too dangerous."

Just then a car pulled up. A man got out. "How do I get to Tigertail Drive?" he asked.

Max opened a map and pointed to the street.

"That will be five cents," he said. "Have you got any more questions, mister?"

"I've always wanted to know where the latissimus dorsi is," the man said very seriously.

Max searched through his books — cookbooks, almanacs, a handbook of chemistry, Roget's *Thesaurus*, and finally an old copy of Gray's *Anatomy*.

"It's this muscle," he said, pointing to a picture.

The man smiled and gave him a quarter. As he drove off, Encyclopedia urged Max not to move his business.

"Half your trade is in finding streets for lost drivers," said the boy detective. "This is the best spot for miles."

"Then I'll sell the business to you," said

ALL KINDS OF
INFORMATION
5¢ to 15¢

Max. "The knowledge in these books is priceless. But for you, Encyclopedia...three dollars."

Suddenly Max lifted his hand to his head in shock at his own words. "Three dollars? Such a deal! I don't believe it myself," he gasped.

"I already have a business," Encyclopedia reminded him. "Now what's so dangerous about this corner?"

"Worn-out sayings," answered Max. "You'll understand. You're bright as a button, not to mention smart as a whip."

"Huh?"

Max explained. His Uncle Bob had sent him a newspaper from Alaska. The newspaper was holding a contest to see what reader could enter the most worn-out sayings, like "flat as a pancake" and "high as a kite."

"I cut the story about the contest from page thirty-one," said Max. "I wrote '*Alaska Times*, page 31' on it in block print. Then I read the rest of the newspaper."

"I'm missing the point," said Encyclopedia.

"There's more," said Max. "I laid the clipping about the contest on this table. I was reading the last page of the newspaper when Bugs Meany came by."

"Bugs! I might have known he was mixed up in this," said Encyclopedia.

Bugs was the leader of a gang of tough older boys called the Tigers. Encyclopedia was kept busy stopping their crooked doings.

Only last week Bugs had filled a glass bowl with water and hung a sign on it: "Invisible Fish. Two Dollars a Pair." Little kids watched for air bubbles and shouted, "There's one!"

Encyclopedia said, "Bugs stole the clipping about the contest?"

"And the newspaper," said Max. "I want to hire you to get back the clipping. Without it, I don't know where to send my list of worn-out sayings."

"Okay," agreed Encyclopedia. "We'll go and see Bugs."

"Not me," said Max. "Bugs is tough as nails, and I've got a thing about living."

"Be brave as a lion and cool as a cucumber," said Encyclopedia. "I've handled Bugs before."

The Tigers' clubhouse was an unused tool shed behind Mr. Sweeny's Auto Body Shop. Bugs was alone when the two boys arrived.

The newspaper story about the contest was tacked to a wall. Encyclopedia wished Max had not used block printing to write the page and name of the newspaper on it. All block printing looked alike.

"You stole my clipping!" accused Max. "There it is on the wall, as big as life!"

"*Stole?*" Bugs hollered at Max. "You're crazy as a bedbug. I *bought* the newspaper from you."

Bugs spread his hands as though asking to be judged from above. "I've lived all my life clean as a whistle and good as gold."

"And you never paid for anything you could steal," said Encyclopedia. "You're tight as a drum and crooked as a dog's hind leg. What would you want with a newspaper from Alaska anyway?"

"I didn't know it was from Alaska until after I bought it," said Bugs. "I saw this kid reading the last page with the story of the contest on it. I wanted the story. I cut it out, marked the page, and tacked it on the wall. Us Tigers are going to win five hundred dollars!"

"I'd be interested in knowing how," snapped Max. "You're dumb as an ox."

"Is that so?" growled Bugs. "When I hit you, you'll lose interest all the way down to the floor."

"Me and my big mouth," Max muttered. "I'm leaving, quiet as a mouse and quick as lightning."

"You're not going anyplace till we get what we came for," said Encyclopedia.

The boy detective turned to Bugs. "You stole Max's newspaper and clipping," he said. "And that is clear as day!"

WHAT MADE ENCYCLOPEDIA
SO SURE?

(Turn to page 65 for the solution to The Case of the Worn-Out Sayings.)

The Case of the Skunk Ape

BUGS MEANY HAD one dream in life. It was to get even with Encyclopedia.

Bugs hated being outsmarted all the time. He dreamed of punching Encyclopedia in the mouth so hard that his eyes would be looking for his teeth.

But Bugs never threw a punch. Whenever he felt like it, he remembered Encyclopedia's junior partner, Sally Kimball.

Sally was not merely the prettiest girl in the fifth grade. She had done what no boy under twelve had thought was possible.

She had knocked Bugs Meany goofy.

Whenever they fought, Bugs ended on the ground, mumbling about the price of yo-yos in China.

Because of Sally, Bugs had quit bullying the boy detective. He never stopped trying to get revenge, however.

"I don't know whom Bugs hates more, you or me," Encyclopedia told Sally. "He'll never live down the lickings you gave him."

Before Sally could answer, Gus Sarmiento rushed into the detective agency. His mouth was open wide enough to swallow a watermelon sideways.

Gus was Idaville's leading boy cello player. Actually, he had first started learning to play the violin. Because of his flat feet, he had switched to the cello. The violin is smaller, but the cello is held between the knees and played sitting down.

"I — I saw it!" he wailed at the detectives. "The Skunk Ape! It reached into my bedroom window!"

The Skunk Ape was Idaville's Abominable Snowman — a creature supposedly half man and half ape.

"I don't believe in Skunk Apes," said Sally. "Did you smell it?"

"I smelled the carpet," answered Gus. "I was so scared I fell on my face." He let out a moan at the memory.

"A hairy arm reached in and grabbed my empty cello case," he said.

"Ha!" said Sally. "A musical Skunk Ape. This I want to see."

Encyclopedia wished Sally weren't always so brave. But he dared not show a yellow streak. He followed her and Gus to Gus's house.

"I was practicing on the cello when I saw the arm," said Gus. "I always practice...between...two and three o'clock...."

His voice trailed off. He had halted outside his bedroom window. In a spot of soft earth was a huge footprint.

Encyclopedia's scalp twitched. "This is my most hair-raising experience since I pulled off my turtleneck sweater," he joked weakly.

"I smell a rat, not a Skunk Ape," said Sally. "Doesn't Wilma Hutton live near here?"

"Three houses down the block," answered Gus.

"She's Bugs Meany's cousin," said Sally. "And she plays the cello!"

Without another word, the three children headed for Wilma's house.

"Look!" said Gus, pointing. A cello case lay among some trees at the side of the garage.

As Gus lifted the case, a car came up the driveway. Wilma Hutton jumped out. She hurried toward the house, taking tripping little steps because of her tight skirt. All the while she screamed, "Police! Police!"

The front door swung open. Out charged Bugs Meany. Behind him was Officer Carlson.

"There's your Skunk Ape, officer!" cried Wilma. "As I drove up, those kids were putting the costume in that cello case."

"That's a dirty lie!" exclaimed Sally.

"Better open the case, Gus," said Officer Carlson.

Gus laid the cello case on the ground and opened it. Inside was an ape costume. The smell made him stagger.

"What died in there?" gagged Bugs.

"Your brain," snapped Sally. "This is a frame-up!"

Bugs clenched his fists and snarled, "May a giant clam bite you on the nose."

"May a sandbag fall on your head," retorted Sally.

"Cool it, you two," said Officer Carlson. "Bugs reported that the Skunk Ape has been frightening his cousin Wilma for days. So I came over to watch for it."

"Wilma can't take much more," Bugs said to the policeman. "She's an artist on the cello. Artists are very high-strung and nervous. That's why they picked on her."

"Oh, that's rich!" said Sally. "She's seventeen and a date with Frankenstein would be laughs. You're just trying to get even, Bugs Meany!"

TIGE

"They knew Wilma's parents are off in Europe," went on Bugs. "Poor girl, she's all alone in this big house. A shock like seeing a Skunk Ape can ruin her career."

"What about mine?" howled Gus.

Officer Carlson waved his hand as a sign for the children to be quiet. "We can get to the bottom of this. Is that your cello case, Gus?"

"It looks like mine," replied Gus. "But a lot of cases look like mine."

"Well, it certainly isn't *mine*," declared Wilma.

She went to her car and opened the trunk. She lifted out a cello case.

"I've been in Glenn City playing the cello," she said. "When I arrived home, I saw these kids among the trees with the Skunk Ape costume. When they saw *me*, they shoved it into the cello case fast."

"Wilma and Bugs are in this together," Sally whispered angrily to Encyclopedia. "I wish I could prove it!"

"You don't have to," replied Encyclopedia. "I can."

WHAT WAS THE CLUE?

(Turn to page 66 for the solution to The Case of the Skunk Ape.)

The Case of the Counterfeit Bill

ARMAND JENKS WAS eight and loved birds. He thought they were nicer than people.

When school let out for the summer, Armand spent his time in the woods. He hardly ever talked. He chirped.

The morning he came into the Brown Detective Agency, however, he wasn't chirping. He was holding a bird's nest.

"The devil has won!" he announced. "Birds are acting like humans — money crazy!"

He laid the nest on the table in front of Encyclopedia. Woven into the lining was a twenty-dollar bill.

"Hopping hoot owls, Armand!" exclaimed Encyclopedia. "Birds can't tell money from a bubble-gum wrapper. Calm yourself. . . ."

Suddenly Encyclopedia was frowning. He had touched the twenty-dollar bill. It felt thin. He got out his magnifying glass.

"This bill is counterfeit," he said. "It doesn't have red and blue fibers."

"Where did you find the nest, Armand?" asked Sally.

"Over in Glenn City," he replied. "There are some good woods behind the old railroad yard."

"Show us the spot," said Encyclopedia.

The children caught the ten-o'clock bus to Glenn City. During the ride, Armand talked sadly about the changes in nature.

"Pretty soon birds won't seek the peace and quiet of the woods anymore," he said.

"Humans have spoiled them," agreed Encyclopedia.

"Birds today go where the action is," said Armand. "I've seen nests lined with match books, mittens, labels from cans, stockings, and pipe cleaners."

"Can you tell where a nest was built just by looking at it?" inquired Encyclopedia.

"Sometimes," said Armand. "I've found nests near a woodworking shop that had wood shavings curled around a few twigs. Tickets are used near theaters, and long hair near beauty parlors."

The bus had reached their stop. The children got off. They walked past the old railroad yard and into the woods.

"Birds have become lazy," said Armand. "They slap together junky nests and grow fat on backyard feeders."

"It's not so bad for them," said Sally. "They have lots more time for themselves."

Armand stopped by a large tree and pointed to a branch.

"That's where I found the nest with the counterfeit bill," he said. "Do you think the counterfeiters are near here?"

"It's possible," said Encyclopedia. He climbed the tree and looked around.

"I can see three houses," he called down. "We'll each take a house and meet back here in half an hour."

The children spread out. Encyclopedia headed for the farthest house.

He approached carefully. As he got near, the front door opened. A man in a policeman's uniform stepped out.

"Can I help you?" he asked pleasantly. He unbuttoned his right breast pocket and pulled out a notebook and pen. Above the pocket was pinned a Glenn City police badge with the number 14.

"I — I lost my way," said Encyclopedia.

He turned and hurried off. Back at the tree, he waited, panting, for the others to return. Armand appeared first.

"Dancing and counterfeiting!" he exclaimed. "They go together!"

As Encyclopedia's jaw dropped, Armand explained.

The front part of the house that he had scouted was a ballet school. A class of small girls was dancing to the music of "The Sugar Plum Fairy." After watching them for a while, he had walked around to a rear window.

"Six women were playing cards in the kitchen!"

"Is that a crime?" inquired Encyclopedia.

"Dancing and cards *lead* to crime," insisted Armand. "Those women start by teaching kids to be graceful. Later, they teach them to pick pockets on tippytoes. After that, gambling and counterfeiting!"

"You'd better go and lie down," muttered Encyclopedia. He was glad to see Sally approaching.

"I got chased by a duck," she said.

She sat down under the tree and told what had happened.

When she had got close to the house she had picked, she heard a loud honking. A big duck charged her.

"A fat man leaned out a window and asked me what I wanted," said Sally. "I said I wanted to get away from the duck."

"Ducks make great watchdogs," piped up Armand.

"The man seemed to be leaving on a trip," continued Sally. "He had a suitcase, a tennis racket, and water skis by the front door. Did you find out anything, Encyclopedia?"

Encyclopedia told her what he and Armand had seen at the other two houses.

"Those women are the counterfeiters," said Armand stubbornly. "They were probably playing cards and betting with counterfeit money when the wind blew the twenty-dollar bill out the window. A bird picked it up and used it to line its nest."

"That might be true," said Sally. "It makes as much sense as anything. But I'm afraid the counterfeiters don't live close by after all."

"I wouldn't be too sure," replied Encyclopedia. "The money isn't the only phony thing around here."

WHAT DID ENCYCLOPEDIA MEAN?

(Turn to page 67 for the solution to The Case of the Counterfeit Bill.)

The Case of the Window Dressers

THE DETECTIVES WERE shopping in Hector's Department Store when Sally's eyes suddenly widened.

"Watch out behind you, Encyclopedia!" she cried. "You're about to be struck by a bull."

Encyclopedia had heard of a bull in a china shop, but never in women's sportswear. Still, he wasn't taking chances. He jumped to his right.

A bull's head with long, curving horns swept by him. It was made of papier-mâché.

"Sorry," apologized a man in shirt sleeves. He hurried on his way, steering the bull's head through the mob of shoppers.

Behind him trailed a parade of slender

young men and women. Sally and Encyclopedia stopped to observe them.

First came four women struggling with the rest of the papier-mâché bull. They were followed by two men carrying bullfighters' costumes and a man with a large color poster of a bullfight.

Next came three more men. Each held a plastic female figure, the kind used in displaying clothes. Bringing up the rear were a man holding several petticoats and a woman with a clothesbrush.

"What's going on?" asked Encyclopedia.

The woman with the clothesbrush lifted her nose. "We are dressing the number seven show window with a display of toreador pants," she answered and strode off.

"Toreador pants?" repeated Encyclopedia. "Who wears them in Idaville?"

"Oh, you males," said Sally disgustedly. "Toreador pants for women are very big this season. They're styled after the pants worn by bullfighters."

Encyclopedia had never seen a bullfight or a show window being dressed. "Let's go watch," he suggested.

The number 7 window was in the front of the store. The area was roped off to keep customers clear.

Sally stood on tiptoes to see over the grown-ups who were lined along the ropes.

"We'd get a better view outside with Red Pufflinger," she said.

Encyclopedia saw Red standing on the side-walk. Red seemed to be staring straight into the window, but his eyes kept crossing.

"My toes hurt," complained Sally after a while. "I'm going outside, where it isn't so crowded, before I need a foot doctor."

"Go outside and you may need an eye doc-tor, like Red," warned Encyclopedia. Never-theless, he followed her.

He didn't get farther than two yards.

Gunshots sounded close by. Women screamed. Shoppers and clerks ran wildly, smashing counters and overturning display cases.

"Hit the floor!" Encyclopedia yelled at Sally. He dropped on his stomach and covered his head with his hands.

The shooting lasted about half a minute. En-cyclopedia recited "The Owl and the Pussy-Cat" to himself before daring to stand up. Sally was gone. Red Pufflinger lay on the sidewalk.

Encyclopedia raced outside. "Red, are you all right?" he cried.

"I'm okay," said Red, rising. "Did you see who fired the shots?"

HECTOR'S

"I thought you could tell me," replied Encyclopedia. "You were looking in."

"I wasn't," said Red. "I was counting."

He explained. He had been using the store window as a mirror to count the freckles on his nose.

"There are two hundred and five," he said proudly. "With the ones on my ears, chin, forehead, and cheeks, I've got two thousand four hundred and seventy. I'm only three short of the championship."

"Wait till next year," mumbled Encyclopedia.

"You know it," said Red. "A teen-ager in Sweetwater is state champ, but he's over the hill. Pimples are ruining him. Next year I'll be champ and win the three-day trip to Whispering Hills for two."

Sirens shrilled. The street came alive with police cars. Several officers, led by Chief Brown, raced into the department store.

Encyclopedia spent the next twenty minutes looking for Sally. He had circled back to the entrance of the store as Chief Brown came out.

"Was anyone hurt, Dad?" asked Encyclopedia.

"No, thank heavens," answered Chief Brown. "A gunman shot up the ceiling. In the confusion, someone stole a hundred thousand dollars' worth of jewelry."

Chief Brown had started for his patrol car when Sally hurried up the street.

"Where have you been?" asked Encyclopedia.

"Chasing crooks," panted Sally. "I figured out who the gunman was and followed him. You know the jewelry department? It's right near the number seven window. As the gunman passed the bracelet counter, two men carrying sacks joined him."

"Then the shooting was simply to scare everyone away from the area," said Chief Brown.

"What a relief," said Red Pufflinger. "For a while I thought the champ from Sweetwater was trying to rub me out!"

"The thieves escaped through the back entrance and jumped into a car," went on Sally. "But I got their license-plate number!"

She handed Chief Brown a slip of paper with the number written on it.

Encyclopedia was dumbfounded. "How did you know who was the gunman?" he said. "I didn't see a gun."

"That," said Sally, "is because you are a boy!"

WHO WAS THE GUNMAN?

(Turn to page 68 for the solution to The Case of the Window Dressers.)

The Case of the Silver Dollar

CHAUNCY VAN THROCKMORTON was the best-dressed boy in Idaville.

He had clothes for every occasion. He put on a riding outfit just to pitch horseshoes.

On the morning he came into the detective agency, however, he wasn't wearing clothes. He was wearing a green towel.

"Chauncy!" said Encyclopedia. "No wonder I didn't hear you approach."

"What are you talking about?" snapped Chauncy.

"I mean..." Encyclopedia checked himself. Chauncy was always showing off by rattling a silver dollar in his pants pocket. He could be heard a block away.

Encyclopedia changed the subject quickly.

"I mean, towels aren't exactly in style for street wear."

"I didn't *want* to wear it," said Chauncy. "I just made a terrible mistake. I fresh-mouthed Lindylou Duckworth."

"Isn't she the seventh grader who's getting up a girls' football team?" asked Sally.

Chauncy nodded. "The girls practice twice a week at South Park. I went there in my new sports jacket to watch. I ended up by running for my life."

He explained. Lindylou had come over to him. The girls were a player short, and she had asked him to fill in.

"I told her that she had only forty cards in her deck if she thought I was going to get my clothes dirty tackling a bunch of knock-knees," said Chauncy. "She got mad and socked me."

His face reddened, and he pointed to a lump over his left eye.

"While I was still dizzy, she dragged me into the woods," he said. "She called me a stuck-up fancy pants and made me undress. Then she asked if I thought I was still so high and mighty. I let my legs do the thinking. I ran."

"*Naked?*" gasped Sally.

"Of course not," said Chauncy. "I had on these green shoes and socks and blue underwear. It was embarrassing."

"I understand," muttered Encyclopedia.

"No, you don't," said Chauncy. "I could have passed for a long-distance runner. But green with blue? The colors — ugh! They clash. It took me a while before I found a nice green towel hanging on a clothesline."

"You have wonderful taste," said Sally.

"It's nothing," replied Chauncy. "What I want now are my clothes. I'll need your help. That Lindylou Duckworth is some kind of monster."

"She is not!" cried Sally. "You're jealous because she's so strong. But we'll help you anyway."

Encyclopedia loaned Chauncy his best shirt and pants, and the three children headed for South Park. On the way, they returned the green towel.

Chauncy walked silently. He didn't have his silver dollar to rattle in his pocket.

Encyclopedia walked silently, too. He wondered how to handle Lindylou, who could pick him up and plant him in the ground.

"A gentleman doesn't fight a lady," thought the boy detective. "I hope Lindylou remembers I'm a gentleman."

The football practice was ending when they reached South Park. Encyclopedia saw Lindylou right away.

She was a blond girl with a pretty face and the broadest shoulders on the field. She was also the only player not wearing shoulder pads.

Sally went straight up to her.

"Chauncy claims you beat him up and took his clothes," she told the bigger girl.

"I don't hit sissies," replied Lindylou. "He did make me mad, though. He stood around watching and rattling his silver dollar."

"How'd you know it was a silver dollar?" demanded Encyclopedia.

"Who doesn't know?" retorted Lindylou. "He was making so much noise I asked him to leave. That's when he took off his clothes."

"I'm having a nightmare," moaned Chauncy.

"You told me you were going to trot a few miles," Lindylou accused Chauncy. "You took off your clothes because you didn't want to get them sweaty."

Lindylou waved at a pile of clothes on the sidelines.

"You left them in a heap right on the field," she said. "I moved them and folded them. No one has touched them but me. So don't you dare say they're wrinkled!"

Encyclopedia followed Chauncy to where his clothes lay on the grass in a neat pile.

"Better check all the pockets," advised Encyclopedia.

Chauncy emptied every pocket. Out came a handkerchief, a sample of tan material for a new suit, the silver dollar, and a leather billfold.

"I had five dollars in my billfold," said Chauncy. "It's gone! And so is eighty cents in change. Lindylou robbed me!"

"Don't talk so loud," warned Encyclopedia. "You'll make her mad."

"I tell you, she's beating her gums off time," whispered Chauncy. "I didn't drop my clothes to run. A lot of the football players must have seen her drag me into the woods."

"They'll say what Lindylou tells them to say," replied Encyclopedia. "Never mind. We don't need witnesses. I know who's lying."

WHO?

(Turn to page 69 for the solution to The Case of the Silver Dollar.)

The Case of the Litterbugs

ENCYCLOPEDIA AND SALLY were walking home from an evening baseball game when they noticed a boy sitting on the curb.

"Gosh," said Sally. "What do you think is bothering him?"

The boy was sitting with his elbow on his knee. His chin rested on his hand.

"That's the saddest-looking boy I ever saw," whispered Encyclopedia.

A big car turned the corner. The driver tossed out an empty cigarette pack and sped off.

The boy looked at the pack lying in the street. Slowly he got to his feet and picked it up. He put it into the trash can on the corner. Then he sat down on the curb again.

Sally walked over to him. "That was a very nice thing you did," she said. "Everyone should do his part to keep our streets clean."

"I used to do more," the boy said, looking up. "I've quit."

"You picked up that pack," Sally reminded him. "So you still care."

"Caring and doing are different," said the boy. He sighed and lowered his chin onto his hand again. "It was such a good idea," he added under his breath.

"What was?" asked Encyclopedia.

"Pride," answered the boy. "I started Pride myself. All the kids from my Sunday School class joined before school let out."

Encyclopedia had heard of Pride. It was the name of a band of children who mailed back litter to the litterbugs during the summer. Their purpose was to keep Idaville beautiful.

"Why did you quit?" asked Sally.

"I got scared," said the boy. "Somebody threatened to fill my belly button with my face if I continued."

"Maybe we can help you," said Encyclopedia. "I'm Leroy Brown and this is Sally Kimball."

"The detectives?" exclaimed the boy. Suddenly he seemed almost cheerful. "I'm Marlo Fosgood. I sure can use help."

"Who threatened you?" asked Encyclopedia.

Marlo took a letter from his pocket. "Here," he said.

Encyclopedia removed the letter from the envelope. He read:

"Dear Marlo Fosgood:

"Stop sticking your nose into other people's trash. If you don't mind this warning, I'm coming after you. I'll shove your face into your belly button."

The letter was typewritten on a plain white sheet. It was not signed, and the envelope had no return address.

"Writing threatening letters is a crime," said Encyclopedia. "Whoever wrote it could go to jail."

"We should give this letter to your father, Encyclopedia," said Sally. "There may be fingerprints on it."

"Unless the guilty person's fingerprints are on file, it wouldn't do any good," said Encyclopedia.

"He probably wore gloves, anyway," said Marlo.

"Can't we do *something*?" said Sally. "Hey, look! On the back of the sheet — there's more typing."

Encyclopedia turned the sheet over. On the

NO
TRASH

back was typed, "The quick brown fox jumped over the lazy dogs."

"That sounds like a line from a book of nursery poems," said Sally, disappointed.

"It isn't," said Encyclopedia. He had closed his eyes. He always did his deepest thinking with his eyes closed. "Tell me, Marlo, how does Pride work?"

"Members mail back litter and include a litter bag," replied Marlo. "The letters we write are kind but firm — a reminder that littering is against the law. We ask the litterbug not to do it again. We get contributions to help cover the cost of the postage."

"How do you know where to mail the litter?" asked Sally.

"Most of the litter returned are envelopes, bills of sale, receipts, and other things with names and addresses on them."

"Suppose there isn't a name or address — like that cigarette pack," said Sally.

"The police help us," answered Marlo. "They trace the license-plate number of the litterbug."

Encyclopedia had opened his eyes. He was studying the postmark on the envelope closely.

"The letter was mailed yesterday in Idaville," he said. "So the person who wrote it must live here."

"And we'd know the typewriter," said Sally. "I mean, no two typewriters write alike. Their letters are sort of like fingerprints."

"That's not much good," said Marlo. "The typewriter could be anyplace in Idaville."

"Can you remember some of the people who got back their litter in the past few days?" inquired Sally.

"No, Pride doesn't keep that kind of records," said Marlo.

"People who write threatening letters are cowards," said Sally in disgust. "This one is a litterbug as well. *Oooh!* Would I like to make him eat his words!"

"So would I," said Marlo. "But we don't know where to find him."

"You're wrong," said Encyclopedia. "The quick brown fox will lead us to him."

HOW?

(Turn to page 70 for the solution to The Case of the Litterbugs.)

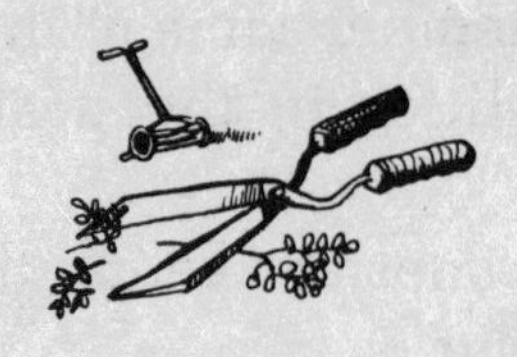

The Case of the Frightened Witness

WHEN SALLY RETURNED to the detective agency after lunch, her first words were, "What does *legible* mean?"

"It means 'able to be read,' " answered Encyclopedia. "What's up?"

"Luther Ginocchio is in some kind of trouble," said Sally. "He's talking funny."

"Luther enjoys using big words like legible," said Encyclopedia. "Sometimes he sounds funny."

Luther Ginocchio was Idaville's leading boy author. He became interested in words while learning to spell his last name.

"It isn't only the big words," said Sally. "You know Bruno Devlin, that bonehead? He's picking on Luther, and I don't know why."

Sally explained. Luther had asked her to

type his latest short story because he didn't have a typewriter. On her way back from lunch, she had stopped at his house with the typewritten story. Luther was cutting the lawn.

"I didn't have a chance to say a word to him before Bruno Devlin ran over," said Sally.

"Bruno lives across the street," said Encyclopedia. "I don't see anything wrong —"

"Neither did I — at first," said Sally. "Bruno stopped behind Luther and stood there as if he wanted to be of help."

Encyclopedia frowned. "Bruno will never get dizzy from doing anyone a good turn."

"I gave Luther back his story," went on Sally. "There wasn't a typing mistake on it. You know all he said? 'It's legible.' Some thanks!"

"What about Bruno?"

"Before Luther had started to speak, Bruno gripped him by the back of the neck," said Sally. "Luther looked scared to death. I asked if Bruno was hurting him."

"Luther said he was fine, of course," guessed Encyclopedia.

"His exact words were, 'Bruno's not my tormentor. I have a headache.' "

Sally lowered her head sheepishly.

"What does *tormentor* mean?"

"It means 'someone who causes suffering,' " replied Encyclopedia.

"Luther was suffering plenty," said Sally. "It

wasn't from a headache. It was from a neck-ache. Bruno was squeezing his neck so hard I thought his feet would swell up."

Suddenly she made a fist.

"This must have something to do with the theft at the elementary school yesterday," she said. "Luther must know something that Bruno doesn't want him to tell!"

Encyclopedia gave the idea some thought. Fifty dollars — five ten-dollar bills — had been stolen from the school office.

"Bruno and Luther have morning jobs at the school," said Sally. "Bruno works in the office. Luther helps Mr. Long, the caretaker, with the grounds."

"You may be on to something," said Encyclopedia. "They both were at the school when the money disappeared."

"Luther wouldn't steal," said Sally. "But Bruno . . . I wonder. He'd throw a drowning man both ends of a rope."

"Mrs. Watts, the assistant principal, came to our house last night," said Encyclopedia. "She told my dad about the theft."

"Did you overhear anything?" asked Sally.

"There wasn't much to overhear," said Encyclopedia. "The money had been left on a desk in the office to pay for a delivery. After the theft, Bruno demanded to be searched to prove his innocence. So did Luther. The money wasn't on either boy."

"Bruno wouldn't demand to be searched unless he had already hidden the money," snorted Sally. "He probably discovered Luther watching him hide it. So Bruno is staying close to Luther till he has a chance to go back for it."

"I think that's the answer," agreed Encyclopedia. "If Luther tells on him, Bruno will beat him up."

"What can we do?" asked Sally worriedly.

"We must get the money before Bruno does," said Encyclopedia. "But we can't let him think Luther squealed. We better get started."

"Where do we begin?" asked Sally. "At the school?"

"At Luther's house," said Encyclopedia. "I want to make sure of the facts."

Luther was clipping the hedge when the two detectives biked up. Bruno was standing beside him like a watchdog.

"Hi, Luther," called Encyclopedia. "Sally says your short story is great. It didn't need one word edited."

At the word 'edited,' Luther's face lit up. He had looked frightened. Now he looked hopeful.

"She did a good job of typing," he said quietly. "And er...er...I'm writing better, too. Do you remember my first story two years ago?"

"It wasn't very good," said Encyclopedia. He picked his next words carefully. "To tell the truth, it smelled worse than an onion."

Luther turned his back on Bruno. A smile flashed across his lips. "Take care," he said, and waved good-bye.

Encyclopedia was halfway down the block before Sally caught up with him.

"Where are you going now?" she asked.

"To the school," replied Encyclopedia. "The money is hidden in one of the classrooms. I would guess in one that is not used during the summer."

"We'll never find it," protested Sally. "You can hide five ten-dollar bills anyplace!"

"It won't be difficult," Encyclopedia assured her. "Check the blackboards. The money is hidden under..."

UNDER WHAT?

(Turn to page 71 for the solution to The Case of the Frightened Witness.)

The Case of the Exploding Plumbing

ENCYCLOPEDIA WAS FINISHING breakfast Saturday morning when Winslow Brant telephoned.

Winslow was Idaville's master snooper. He snooped around in the city dump and the neighborhood trash piles. Whenever he found junk that was worth keeping, he fixed it up and sold it as an antique.

He wasn't calling about antiques, however. He was calling about his life.

"You'd better get to my place quick!" he said. "I was nearly killed by my toilet!"

Encyclopedia didn't waste time with questions. "I'll be right over," he said.

Winslow lived nine blocks away in an apartment house. He was waiting out in front when Encyclopedia arrived.

The detective got off his bike as a small station wagon stopped at the curb. It was jammed with all kinds of junk. There wasn't room left to fit anything larger than a pencil among the mess of old dishes, lamps, glassware, and whatnots.

The driver, Gladys Smith, was eighteen and a junk collector like Winslow. She seemed surprised to see him standing in front of the apartment house.

"Is everything all right, Winslow?" she called.

"Everything except my toilet," answered Winslow.

Two fire trucks pulled up. Firemen raced into the building.

"We'd better use the back entrance," said Winslow. He motioned Encyclopedia and Gladys to follow him. He went around to the rear, through the parking lot, and into the service elevator.

"I flushed the toilet and it started to make funny noises," he said. "Hot water shot up. So I ran. Then the toilet exploded."

The elevator stopped at the sixth floor. Winslow opened the door of his apartment. "Don't worry, Mom," he shouted. "Encyclopedia Brown is here."

His mother was sitting dazedly in the living

room. His father was at the telephone asking questions about insurance. The floors were soaked, and water was dripping from the ceilings.

"This way," said Winslow. He walked into the bathroom. Nothing was left of the toilet but pipes and little white pieces.

"Boy, am I glad I ran," he said.

"This is just terrible," said Gladys. "But we'd better get started, Winslow."

"Gladys is driving me up to Cedartown," Winslow said to Encyclopedia. "The biggest antique market of the year is being held there today. I have a lot of things to sell."

"I'll help you carry them to my car," said Gladys.

"They're in two orange crates in the boiler room," said Winslow. "My folks won't let me store anything in the apartment. What about the toilet, Encyclopedia? Was it a bomb?"

"I don't know yet," answered Encyclopedia.

He went to the window. Winslow's apartment faced the rear of the building. The detective stared down at the parking lot.

"I want to see the boiler room," he said.

Two firemen and the building's handyman were in the boiler room. The handyman told Winslow he could take his boxes of antiques, but to be careful. The floor was covered with water.

"Golly," said Winslow uneasily. "I hope my antiques are all right."

His orange crates were split apart. Everything inside them was smashed.

"My lion...!" whimpered Winslow.

While he fought back tears, Gladys explained about the lion.

Two weeks ago, she and Winslow had found two small marble lions in a garage sale. They were ugly, but they looked rare and old and so might be worth a lot of money.

"Winslow bought one, and I bought the other," she told Encyclopedia. "We were going to have them checked by an expert at the antique sale today."

Encyclopedia nodded and moved about the pipes and tanks of the boiler room. In the corner he saw a pickax, a shovel, and a sledgehammer. He showed the sledgehammer to Winslow.

"The person who smashed all your antiques also exploded your toilet," the detective said. "Probably with this."

Winslow looked at the sledgehammer questioningly.

"The guilty person was swinging it at your antiques when it slipped," said Encyclopedia. "It smashed this — the central coil within these two heat exchangers."

The firemen and the handyman stopped talking. They stepped closer to Encyclopedia and stood listening.

"With the heat exchangers broken, the boiling water from the central heating plant escaped into the regular hot- and cold-water pipes," said Encyclopedia.

"Of course!" said the handyman. "That would cause the copper sweat joints in the pipes to soften and pull apart clear to the top floor."

"And where the joints didn't break," said one of the firemen, "the hot water shot into the cold porcelain bowls and tanks and shattered them."

"Say," declared the handyman, his voice full of wonder. "You're some smart little kid."

"But who would want to smash all Winslow's lovely antiques?" protested Gladys.

"You," said Encyclopedia.

HOW DID ENCYCLOPEDIA KNOW?

(Turn to page 72 for the solution to The Case of the Exploding Plumbing.)

The Case of the Salami Sandwich

ZIGGY KETCHUM WAS sixteen and the most absentminded boy in Idaville.

He often hired Encyclopedia to help him find things. Only last month Ziggy lost his wristwatch. Encyclopedia found it on his other wrist.

Early Friday morning Ziggy entered the Brown Detective Agency. He laid a quarter on the gas can.

"I want to hire you," he said. "I'm going to lose my job."

"Good grief, Ziggy," exclaimed Encyclopedia. "We can't help you find something you haven't lost yet!"

"Well, if you find my lunch, I won't lose my job."

While Encyclopedia blinked his eyes, Ziggy explained.

During the summer he worked in Hector's Department Store. Every day he hid his lunch in a different box of boys' shoes.

"I forgot where I hid my lunch — a salami sandwich — Monday. If Mr. Wilson, the floor manager, finds it before I do, I'm dead."

"Why do you have to hide your lunch?" asked Sally.

"Al Noshman is the other stock boy on the third floor," said Ziggy. "If I don't hide my lunch, he eats it."

"He must be fast with the teeth," said Encyclopedia.

"Fast as lightning," said Ziggy. "He eats his dessert with his soup spoon."

"You should go to a restaurant for lunch," said Encyclopedia.

"Naw, it costs too much," said Ziggy.

"Al Noshman should at least take you out to eat now and then," said Sally. "He owes it to you."

"He took me to the Dog Shack last week," admitted Ziggy. "I'll never go again."

"Why not?" inquired Sally. "Didn't he pay the check?"

"He paid," replied Ziggy. "But he said terrible things like: 'This tablecloth is filthy — has it come straight off the bed?' 'Do you run your own hospital for people who eat here?' It was awful."

"It could have been worse," said Encyclopedia. "Al forgot to ask, 'When did the waiters go on strike?' and 'Do you kill your own garbage here?'"

"He probably said those things on purpose," suggested Sally, "so you wouldn't want to go out to eat with him again."

The detectives discussed what to do. They decided to go with Ziggy to Hector's Department Store and search the stock room for the salami sandwich. They took the number 3 bus into town.

Ziggy went into the store by the employees' entrance. Encyclopedia and Sally waited on the street until ten o'clock, when the doors opened. They met Ziggy on the third floor.

Home furnishings took up half the floor, and men's and boys' clothing the other half. Ziggy pointed to a door at each end of the floor.

"Those doors lead to the stock rooms," he said. "Al Noshman handles home furnishings. I take care of clothing. Follow me."

The children walked slowly through the clothing department. It was filled with every kind of men's and boys' wear, from caps to shoes.

Sally gasped as they entered the stock room. "There must be five hundred shoe boxes, plus a zillion others!"

"I've been working here a month," said Ziggy. "I still haven't learned half the colors and sizes."

"We'll never be able to look through all the boxes without being caught," said Sally.

"How do you remember which shoe box you put your lunch into?" asked Encyclopedia.

"I make a list for each week," said Ziggy. He took a piece of paper from his pocket.

On it he had written: "Brown 7½, Brown 7, White 7½, Tan 6, White 6½." After each color and size was a check.

"The check means I found my lunch for that day," said Ziggy. "This is last week's list."

"Then all we have to do is look at this week's list," said Sally.

Ziggy shook his head. "I made up a new list on Monday. Last Monday I took sick with fever and had to quit early. I forgot about my lunch, and I don't remember where I put the new list."

"Do you have a locker in the store?" asked Encyclopedia.

"Downstairs," said Ziggy. "Say, you've got the smarts! I remember now—I put this week's list on the shelf."

Sandals
Heather
Sweaters

He dashed off and returned waving a slip of paper. He showed it to Encyclopedia.

The boy detective read: "Black 6, Black 6½, Tan 7¼, Red 7¾, Natural 7½." There wasn't a check on the sheet.

"Black size six!" sang Ziggy. "It won't take me long to get the salami sandwich now. You two better move before Mr. Wilson, the floor manager, finds you in here."

The detectives slipped onto the selling floor and waited for Ziggy by a rack of men's ties.

Presently Ziggy came out of the stock room. He walked toward the rack as if he were going to use a tie to hang himself.

"I've looked through every box of size six black shoes," he said. "No salami sandwich. I must have been sicker than I thought when I made up the list Monday. If Mr. Wilson finds my lunch in with a pair of shoes, I can start hunting for a new job."

"Don't worry," said Encyclopedia. "I know where to find the sandwich."

WHERE?

(Turn to page 73 for the solution to The Case of the Salami Sandwich.)

Solution to

The Case of the Runaway Elephant

Mr. Hunt never paid for the elephant.

He lied when he said Mr. Xippas refused to accept payment on Friday the thirteenth because it was bad luck.

But what tripped him up was another lie. He said he had gone to the bank on April Fools' Day and had drawn out the money to buy Jimbo. Impossible!

Because it happened seventeen years ago, he thought he was safe. He had not reckoned on Encyclopedia.

April Fools' Day is April 1.

As Encyclopedia knew, if in any month a Friday falls on the thirteenth, the first day of the month is Sunday.

On Sundays banks are closed.

Solution to
The Case of the Worn-Out Sayings

Both Max and Bugs claimed to have written "*Alaska Times*, p. 31" on the story about the contest.

Since the writing was in block letters, Encyclopedia could not tell who was speaking the truth.

But Bugs said he had first noticed the story about the contest on the last page of the newspaper. That was his mistake!

The last page of a newspaper is never an odd number like 31. The last page is always an even number, like 30, or 18, or 42.

Foiled again, Bugs gave back the clipping.

Max entered the contest, tied for forty-third prize, and won a ballpoint pen.

Solution to *The Case of the Skunk Ape*

Bugs got Officer Carlson to wait in Wilma's house during the time Gus always practiced the cello.

Meanwhile, Wilma dressed as the Skunk Ape and stole the cello case. Then she rubbed the costume with rotten eggs, stuffed it into the case, and left the case where it could be easily found.

Bugs knew Gus would run to Encyclopedia for help. When the children found the cello case, Wilma was watching from her parked car. She drove up the driveway and then hurried toward the house in her tight skirt.

Encyclopedia realized that she could not have just come home from playing the cello, as she claimed.

A cello is held between the knees. A woman wears pants or a loose skirt — never a *tight* skirt — to play it!

Solution to
The Case of the Counterfeit Bill

Encyclopedia telephoned his father and told him about the counterfeit bill and the policeman.

Chief Brown called the Glenn City chief of police. It was quickly discovered that one uniform and badge number 14 had been stolen from the police storeroom.

The house was raided. A million dollars in counterfeit bills was found. And four of the gang were captured, including the fake policeman.

What had made Encyclopedia suspicious?

A policeman *always* wears his badge over his heart — on his left breast.

The fake policeman had forgotten. He had pinned his badge on his right breast.

Solution to
The Case of the Window Dressers

Sally realized who the gunman was: the man who didn't belong in the parade of window dressers.

The window was being dressed to display toreador pants. As every girl knows, petticoats are worn under skirts, not under pants.

So the man carrying the petticoats was not really a window dresser. He had scooped up some petticoats from a store counter and used them to hide the gun.

While everyone fled for their lives, the gunman's two partners robbed the jewelry department.

Because Sally had written down the license number of their getaway car, the three robbers were captured and the jewelry was recovered.

Solution to *The Case of the Silver Dollar*

Lindylou Duckworth said that she had asked Chauncy to leave the field because he was making so much noise rattling his silver dollar.

She also said that nobody had touched his clothes but she herself. That made her the thief!

When Chauncy emptied his pockets, he found the silver dollar, but no change. He could not have rattled the silver dollar against the soft objects in his pocket.

Trapped by her own words, Lindylou admitted she had been lying.

She had stolen the eighty cents, plus the five dollars from his billfold, after moving his clothes from the woods.

She returned the money. And Chauncy never insulted girl football players again.

Solution to *The Case of the Litterbugs*

"The quick brown fox jumped over the lazy dogs" was Encyclopedia's clue.

The sentence uses every letter in the alphabet.

The person who wrote it, Encyclopedia realized, was testing his typewriter. So he either had just bought it, or he had had an old one repaired.

Encyclopedia told his father. Chief Brown checked with the stores that sold or repaired typewriters. He got the names of everyone who had recently bought a typewriter or who had had an old one repaired.

The police were able to match the typing on the letter with the typewriter belonging to Duke Kelly, one of Bugs Meany's Tigers.

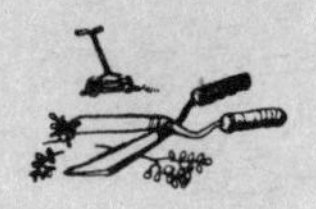

Solution to
The Case of the Frightened Witness

When Sally dropped off the typewritten story, Luther gave her three clues: the words "legible," "tormentor," and "headache."

Sally repeated to Encyclopedia what Luther had said, as Luther hoped she would. Encyclopedia caught the clues, but went to see Luther in order to be sure.

He was sure when Luther's face lit up at the word "edited," and when Luther smiled at the word "onion."

"Legible," "tormentor," "headache," "edited," and "onion" all have one thing in common. The last letters of each word are the same as the beginning letters.

So Encyclopedia went back to the school. He found the money hidden on a blackboard shelf, under an eraser.

Solution to
The Case of the Exploding Plumbing

Gladys smashed all Winslow's antiques in order to hide the fact that she was interested only in the lion.

With Winslow's lion smashed, her lion would be more valuable. As the only one in existence, it would be worth more money.

But Gladys was *too* greedy. She loaded too many of her own antiques into her station wagon to sell at the Cedartown market. There wasn't room for Winslow's!

She could not have known Winslow would not be taking his antiques unless she was the one who had smashed them!

Since Winslow's apartment faced the parking lot in the rear, she had parked in front. She didn't want him to see her overloaded wagon.

She hadn't expected to find him in front with Encyclopedia. Winslow didn't notice anything wrong. But Encyclopedia did!

Solution to

The Case of the Salami Sandwich

To keep Al Noshman from finding his lunch, Ziggy hid it in a different shoe box every day.

"I still haven't learned half the colors and sizes," he admitted. That was his problem!

His new week's list of hiding places read: "Black 6, Black 6½, Tan 7¼, Red 7¾, Natural 7½."

Encyclopedia knew that shoes aren't made in sizes ending in fractions like ¼ and ¾. But hats — and caps, which the department sold — are!

On Monday, the sick and absentminded Ziggy had hidden his lunch in a box of size six black caps!

Thanks to Encyclopedia. Ziggy recovered his sandwich and saved his job.

About the Author

Donald J. Sobol was born in New York City and attended Oberlin College in Oberlin, Ohio. After serving with the U.S. Army Combat Engineers in the Pacific Theater during World War II, he worked on the editorial staffs of the *New York Sun* and the *Long Island Daily Press*.

A writer for more than 25 years, he has written fifty books, including fifteen *Encyclopedia Brown* mysteries. He now lives in Miami, Florida with his family and enjoys scuba diving and restoring antique cars.

About the Illustrator

Leonard Shortall has written and illustrated over 17 books and has illustrated more than 70 books by various authors, including many *Encyclopedia Brown* mysteries by Donald J. Sobol.

Born in Seattle, Washington, he attended the University of Washington and has worked in advertising. He is married and has three children.